P.B. BEAR

The Pajama Party

Lee Davis

FAMILY LEARNING

One day P.B. Bear and his friends were playing dress up at his house. "Vroom, vroom," zoomed Hilda. "Treasure ahoy!" shouted Dermott. "Charge!" Roscoe galloped on his horse. "Lights, camera, action!" sang Franny, flicking her golden wig in the air. "Look at me. I'm a superbear!" said P.B. Bear, racing around the living room.

Suddenly P.B. Bear ran past the clock on the mantlepiece. "Oh, no!" he cried, holding it up. "We were having so much fun we didn't notice how late it is!"

The friends all ran to the window and looked out.
"It's dark outside," said Roscoe.
"And I'm afraid of the dark."
"It's raining," said Hilda. "I hate getting wet."
"I hear thunder," said Dermott.
"I'm scared of loud noises."
"What are we going to do?" asked Franny.
"I know," said P.B. Bear. "You can all spend
the night at my house. That way nobody
will have to go out in the dark, get wet,
or be alone with the thunder."
"Yes, please!" cried the friends.

"What about pajamas?" asked Roscoe.

"I'm the only one who has to wear pajamas," said P.B., "because I'm Pajama Bedtime Bear. Everyone else can stay in their dress-up clothes."

"Yeah!" said Roscoe. "I can be a knight all night long!"

P.B. Bear put on his pajamas, then added his mask, his belt, and his cape. "Look, everyone, Super Pajama Bedtime Bear is ready for bed."

"But where are we going to sleep?" asked Hilda.

"I don't think there is enough room in your bed for all of us," said Franny.

"No," said Dermott, shaking his head.

"Don't worry," said P.B. "I'll find a special place for each of you."

P.B. Bear looked around his room. "Roscoe, you can borrow my sleeping bag, and sleep right next to my bed." "And my horse can sleep right next to me," said Roscoe. "Good idea," said P.B. Bear. "Here, take my flashlight. Then you won't be scared of the dark."

"Thanks, P.B.!" said Roscoe.

"What about me?" asked Hilda.

"Hmm," thought P.B. Bear. "You need a dry nest."

"You could sleep on the windowsill," suggested Franny.

"Oh, no," said Hilda. "That's too close to the rain.
Vroom, vroom . . . I'll sleep here high up on
P.B.'s chest of drawers where I won't get wet."

"Where do you want to sleep, Franny?" asked P.B. Bear.
"How about in this basket?"
"Oh, no," said Franny.
"Actresses can't sleep
in *baskets*. I want to sleep
in a hammock."

"We could use this scarf to make you one," said Hilda.
So she helped P.B. Bear and Franny string up a
hammock between the bed and the chest of drawers.
Franny hopped in. "Ahh," she said, "just right."
"What about Dermott?" asked P.B. Bear,
looking around his room. "Where could he sleep?"
"Oh," they all said at once. "Where is Dermott?"

The friends looked everywhere in P.B. Bear's room.
They looked on top of the bookshelf, in the toy box,
under the comforter, behind the bedside table . . .

. . . until at last P.B. Bear cried, "Here he is! He's hiding from the thunder!"

Dermott opened one eye, grunted, and rolled over.
"Shhh!" whispered the friends. "Time for bed."

So they all snuggled down to
sleep in their special beds.
"Good night!" called P.B. Bear.
"Good night, P.B.,"
whispered his friends.